BIG GREEN POETRY MACHINE

The Power Of Words

Edited By Briony Kearney

First published in Great Britain in 2023 by:

Young Writers
Remus House
Coltsfoot Drive
Peterborough
PE2 9BF
Telephone: 01733 890066
Website: www.youngwriters.co.uk

All Rights Reserved
Book Design by Ashley Janson
© Copyright Contributors 2023
Softback ISBN 978-1-80459-522-0

Printed and bound in the UK by BookPrintingUK
Website: www.bookprintinguk.com
YB0541S

FOREWORD

Welcome Reader,

For Young Writers' latest competition The Big Green Poetry Machine, we asked primary school pupils to craft a poem about the world. From nature and environmental issues to exploring their own habitats or those of others around the globe, it provided pupils with the opportunity to share their thoughts and feelings about the world around them.

Here at Young Writers our aim is to encourage creativity in children and to inspire a love of the written word, so it's great to get such an amazing response, with some absolutely fantastic poems. It's important for children to be aware of the world around them and some of the issues we face, but also to celebrate what makes it great! This competition allowed them to express their hopes and fears or simply write about their favourite things. The Big Green Poetry Machine gave them the power of words and the result is a wonderful collection of inspirational and moving poems in a variety of poetic styles.

I'd like to congratulate all the young poets in this anthology; I hope this inspires them to continue with their creative writing.

CONTENTS

Arc Oakbridge School, Birmingham

Poppy Zarifeh (11)	1
Macheo King-Brown (11)	2

Barnhill Primary School, Broughty Ferry

Rebecca Sharpe (11)	3
Jessica Donald (11)	4
Islay Crowe (11)	6

Bright Futures School, Lymm

Holly Snook (7)	8

Brighton Avenue Primary School, Gateshead

Bernice Nwaugo (10)	9
Matthew Cousins (9)	10
Nathan Chakwawa (9)	11
Sagnik Mandal (10)	12
Ethan Dubre (9)	13

Clyst Heath Nursery & Community Primary School, Clyst Heath

Penny Onslow (11)	14
Sofia Blell (8)	15
Lola Arfan (10)	16
Maddison Porter (7)	17
Cerys Lloyd (10)	18
Ezra Dew (7)	19
Tymon Nadolny (8)	20

Gabriella Reece (10)	21
Amie Davey (8)	22
Phoebe Rutter (8)	23
Alice Kachali (9)	24
Taylor Scholfield (9)	25
Poppy Morgan (7)	26
Rory Hart (8)	27
Gabriella Booth (7)	28
Sebastian Czapiewski (8)	29
Alex Weissabel (8)	30
Sophia Axon (10)	31
Marley Gould (7)	32
Olivia Holingworth (8)	33
Ted Elmer (6)	34
Ellie Pallister (6)	35
Oliver Ernest (7)	36
Francesca Balch (5)	37

Cwmaber Junior School, Abertridwr

Ruby Jenkins (10)	38
Corin Williams-Baker (11)	39
Megan Davies (8)	40
Alexa Davies (11)	41
Gracie Davies (10)	42
Evie Williams (11)	43
Lowri Harding (9)	44
Seren Humphreys (8)	45
Hyrum Perry (8)	46
Gracie Gould (10)	47
Freddie Evans (9)	48
Kian Hart (11)	49
Evie Carben (7)	50
Summer Smith Harris (8)	51

Garway Primary School, Garway

Libby Williams (8)	52
Sophie Nicholls (9)	54
Lena Sparey (8)	56
Florence Fullbrook (8)	58
Alfred Simpson (8)	60
Albert Simpson (8)	62
Cordelia Siriwardena (8)	64
Charlie Myhil (8)	66
Isla Woodhouse (7)	68
Teddy Fullbrook (6)	69
Annabel Atkinson (9)	70
Louis Moulton (7)	71
Aden Evans (10)	72
Reuben Hill (9)	74
Thea Probert (6)	75
Samuel Gwenter (9)	76
Aiden Read (11)	77
Olive Johnson (9)	78
Mabel Jones (9)	79
Ottilie Learmond (7)	80
Malakai Longden Berg (9)	81
Ludo Probert (6)	82
Samuel Rusling (9)	83
Nicole Evans (6)	84
William Franklin (10)	85
Ebenie Barreau (11)	86
Ronnie Monaghan-Teale (9)	87
Libby Quan (7)	88
Jack Monaghan-Teale (11)	89
Rachel Pugh (9)	90
Greta Hoare-Shields (7)	91
Henry Morgan (10)	92
Reuben Littler (7)	93
Harriet Plant (10)	94
Daniel Caleb Evans (11)	95
Thomas Hughes (10)	96
Rosie Christopher (6)	97
Edward Morris (10)	98
Angelo-Valentino Cable (11)	99
Molly Siriwardena (11)	100
Layla Carter (11)	101
James Peacock (11)	102
Jacob Pugh (11)	103
Gene Farr (10)	104
Jacks Sparey (7)	105
Kayleigh Cobourn (10)	106
Nerys Gwenter (6)	107
Poppy Brown (9)	108

Haughton St Giles CE Primary Academy, Haughton

Vesper (8)	109

Holy Trinity CE Junior School, Wallington

Abdullah Saud Mannan (10)	110
Maximilian Zatik (10)	111
Daisy Davies (10)	112
Finley Styles (10)	114
Sam Hunter-Brook (9)	115
Jack Walton (10)	116
Robyn Lang (10)	118
Betina Khoobyar (10)	119
Sydney-Rose Still-Hibbert (10)	120
Jasmine D'Souza (9)	121
Abrar Gamaleldin (10)	122
Ethan Vass (9)	123
Felix White (10)	124
Ava Brook (10)	125
Lillian Katat Cheetham (9)	126
Beatrice Merivale (10)	127
Mohamad Sidibe (10)	128
Emily-Rose Tindle (9)	129
Nysa Ray (9)	130

Prince Edward Primary School, Sheffield

Toochi Nwagbo (9)	131
Esther Nwagbo (10)	132
Chimamanda Okoroafor (8)	135
Amen Messam (5)	136
Praise Shodeinde (10)	137

Rokeby School, Kingston Upon Thames

Ruben Thurairatnam (8)	138

Shocklach Oviatt CE Primary School, Malpas

Niamh Hirst (9)	139
Sophie Lloyd (11)	140
Sophia Whittle-Jones (10)	142
Eve Goggins (10)	143
Annabel Burnett (10)	144
Eva Nicholas (9)	145
Elliot Williams (8)	146

St Nicholas CE Primary School, Henstridge

Amy Kingdon (8)	147
George Morgan (7)	148
Maisie Bartlett (9)	149
Scarlett Ricketts (7)	150
Maddie Elliott (8)	151
Jake Stanley (9)	152
Alfie Mckenna (8)	153
Scarlett Moore (8)	154
Summer Groves (7)	155
Logan Sunley (8)	156
James Sparshott (7)	157
Kenny Smith (8)	158
Esme Morris (8)	159
Lucas Cole (7)	160
Freddie Windsor (7)	161
Ronny Whitney (8)	162
Iesha Peckover (7)	163
Isaac George New (8)	164
Mckenzie Murphy (8)	165
Toby Bowden (8)	166
Grace Windsor (9)	167
Samuel Hardie (8)	168
Oliver Moult (7)	169
Alyssa Mortley (7)	170
Archie Parsons (8)	171

Jimmy Hughes (7)	172
E Hancock (8)	173

The Mount School, York

Agnes Obi (10)	174
Phoebe Murgatroyd (10)	176
Clementine Myatt (10)	177

Widmer End Pre School, Widmer End

Imogen R (8)	178

Woolston Brook School, Padgate

Morgan Birchall (11)	179
Riley Byrne (8)	180
Olivia Parkes (8)	181

Our World

D o you know about plants and animals? Do you know that the planet is failing that holds you and me?
R emember happiness, remember peace, remember love and harmony,
E verybody in the world, boys and girls, are trying to stop this great calamity,
A nd because of that, we all try so hard, but still this planet is falling apart,
M aybe if they stop to listen, then maybe this planet that holds us would not be falling apart.

Poppy Zarifeh (11)
Arc Oakbridge School, Birmingham

Nature

N ature is emerald,
A lways recycle,
T rees look green and important,
U nbelievable Earth,
R eal, rapid, rushing river,
E co-warriors stand up.

Macheo King-Brown (11)
Arc Oakbridge School, Birmingham

The Old To New Ocean

I can remember the sea,
It was a wonderful place,
But now I must plea,
That I don't consume a shoelace.

As I glide through the ocean,
I feel it's just a cursed potion,
Wherever I go,
There's rubbish, I know.

The common plastic bottle
Is really, really awful,
Even a tiny bottle cap
Could be an evil trap.

The old sea was much better,
It felt much safer,
The new sea feels like a fetter,
And feels like a broken wafer.

Rebecca Sharpe (11)
Barnhill Primary School, Broughty Ferry

The Beauty In Nature

Nature is our treasure,
And yet we throw it about at our pleasure,
Nature is our safety and home,
And yet we still see plastic roam,
Nature would never look at us all snooty,
And so you would think looking after it would be our duty,
That's why I write this poem to show its beauty.

I must begin with the sun,
And how, when it comes out, happiness is won,
Or how it blossoms our flowers,
Or how it brightens the hours,
In our coldest moments, it keeps us warm,
It keeps us optimistic when sadness seems to form,
When it gleams, so do our hearts,
And so, the sun is like a work of art.

Of course, we must include snow,
And how, when it appears, gleefulness seems to grow,
It brings people together,

Though I guess that's expected for such beautiful weather,
It's comforting and peaceful,
And also makes you feel easeful,
So, my tip for you is to go put on your gloves,
And experience the love.

Let's not forget about storms,
And how, when it strikes, amenity seems to form,
It creates memories that will forever last,
Even in fifty years when you look back on your past,
It creates an amazing sensation,
That will never be rationed,
So, go cosy up and I will make a bet,
You'll make memories you'll never forget.

Do you now see the beauty in nature?
And how much it's worth?
But not in price,
Instead, a love that is so nice,
I hope you see it now,
And if not, then, wow!

Jessica Donald (11)
Barnhill Primary School, Broughty Ferry

The World I Love In My Eyes

This is our world, a world worth saving,
No Planet B to save us now,
We will save this world, some way, somehow,
A world I greatly wish to be freed,
A sadness I wish of only to read,
An underwater world it may be,
A sadness among our beautiful seas,
A living creature in the tree,
I wish to save this beautiful place,
A planet that roams with amazing grace,
A woeful wolf as it cries,
Watching his planet as it dies,
A blissful bear from up north,
Wishing for mortals to open their eyes,
And see its world as it dies,
Horse and carriage in our past,
Our world being killed by things moving fast,
A fire burning, smoke in our air,
The smoke that you see cares for nobody,

Killing our trees, killing our seas,
Let this world finally be free,
For this is the world I love in my eyes.

Islay Crowe (11)
Barnhill Primary School, Broughty Ferry

Help Our World

Help our world,
Plant more trees,
Plant more flowers,
Help our world.

Holly Snook (7)
Bright Futures School, Lymm

Fatherhood

At first,
I arise and shine at dawn,
My little daughter tells me to brush her teeth,
I brush it,
My little daughter wants to eat pancakes,
I make it,
My little daughter wants me to take her to school,
I take her.

But now,
My little girl doesn't want me to brush her teeth anymore,
I won't do it,
My little girl doesn't want me to walk her to school anymore,
I understand,
My little girl prefers I stay at home more,
I stay,
It dawned on me,
My little girl isn't so little anymore.

Bernice Nwaugo (10)
Brighton Avenue Primary School, Gateshead

What We Should Do With The Earth

All the animals that have died,
And are now extinct because of pollution and climate change,
We need to help Earth,
Recycle plastic,
And save the rainforests,
Save nature!
Protect the environment before humans go extinct,
Even if it isn't your dream,
Recycle all of the plastic you don't use,
Say you were a tree or any sort of nature,
The Earth and nature get polluted
With all the stuff people don't put in the bin,
So all of these reasons are good reasons to help the Earth.

Matthew Cousins (9)
Brighton Avenue Primary School, Gateshead

Climate Change

The world we are living in
Needs us to look after it,
The Earth where living things are,
Things need to be looked after,
E.g. soil, water, trees, grass, mountains, rivers, oceans,
Trees make up rainforests,
Every living thing needs water,
E.g. humans, animals, trees, grass,
They all need water,
So, all living things need a good environment,
We need to stop pollution,
Everybody needs to recycle materials.

Nathan Chakwawa (9)
Brighton Avenue Primary School, Gateshead

The Blue Conundrum

I am the sea,
I am brave and mighty,
Ships come bobbing up and down,
I make sailors lose their bravery,
Ships come without fear,
My anger no longer bears,
I make a wave, big and high,
Whoosh! They're gone, out of sight,
And now you stand before me,
Full of determination,
Could it be, just maybe,
I'll let you have your day.

Sagnik Mandal (10)
Brighton Avenue Primary School, Gateshead

The Things I See

All the things you see are fabulous,
Like a tin can or a bee,
Look around you, what do you see?
The walls, the floors, the roof,
It's fabulous,
But the thing I really love,
Is a new pair of shoes,
A new pair of shoes made of leather,
Thread and laces,
All out of nature,
Nature is really wonderful.

Ethan Dubre (9)
Brighton Avenue Primary School, Gateshead

The Plastic Giant And The Nature Giant

The plastic giant, whom everyone hates,
Carries a big plastic rake,
She uses it to smash up things,
Our toys, our cars, our phones that ring,
When this happens, she'll laugh and say,
"I'm big, you're small,
And there is nothing you can do, nothing at all!"
But then, one day, at the smashing hour,
The plastic giant came back... with a flower,
Next to her, to their utter surprise,
Was another giant, with shining pink eyes,
Then he turned to face the other giant,
"Stop," he said, and she dropped her rake,
"Stop this mess, for heaven's sake!"
So now the giants, together they stand,
Trying to stop people littering the land,
The moral of this is simple indeed,
That there is no Planet B!

Penny Onslow (11)
Clyst Heath Nursery & Community Primary School, Clyst Heath

Nature Matters

N ature creates happiness for people on Earth,
A nd even the gloomiest of people can feel its warmth,
T ourists travel worlds to find a forest or two,
U nder trees, there will be...
R ed and orange foxes lurking around the shadows,
E ndless butterflies dancing in the magical jungle,

M ake pollution disappear,
A lways listen to Mother Nature's guide,
T hink before extinct,
T ake a moment to think of what you could do to make the Earth a better place,
E ven if you don't love it, always try to enjoy it,
R est in peace, I'll tell all of the plants and wildlife that died long ago,
S leep in harmony too, if the people don't bother you!

Sofia Blell (8)
Clyst Heath Nursery & Community Primary School, Clyst Heath

Recycle

Once you've finished your yoghurt and juice,
The plastic inside doesn't bring you much use,
After you've finished your lunch at school,
Recycling more does really feel cool,
You finally get your fancy new shoes,
Recycle the box and there's nothing to lose,
You use so much foil, roll it into a ball,
Go green today, it is better for all,
Recycle the drink cans that you had today,
Who knows? They might fly you on holiday,
Your recycling might turn into a plane,
Or it might just stay the same,
The bin is just waiting, a few steps away,
So go ahead and recycle, recycle today.

Lola Arfan (10)
Clyst Heath Nursery & Community Primary School, Clyst Heath

Robin

R obin, red as rubies, robin, red breast on your chest, you sit so peaceful, like a silent snail, meticulously you catch a worm, but once it's in your mouth, one blink and it's gone!
O bserving worms, robin is so silent, you're like a dormouse, your breast is fire, your beak is chocolate, and underneath your finery is a hidden ghost,
B rown bark on the branch you're sitting on, wriggly worm pink head to toe,
I nteresting to watch the worm wriggle and squirm, now fly to rest, white eggs with red speckles on,
N o one is as grand at worm-catching as robin, for robin is a mighty oak tree!

Maddison Porter (7)
Clyst Heath Nursery & Community Primary School, Clyst Heath

Our World

O ur world is our home and it is our job to protect it and its inhabitants,
U pcycling things is a great way to start recycling,
R enewable energy is wind, water, and the sun, it helps to stop climate change,

W orking together is the only way we can save Earth and the life cycle,
O ur planet needs us, just like we need it, so we are there for it,
R ainforests are being cut down and animals are losing their habitats,
L ife, to live we need the world and the world needs us, we work together,
D ream big, act bold to save, heal, and protect our world.

Cerys Lloyd (10)
Clyst Heath Nursery & Community Primary School, Clyst Heath

Our World

I like the way you can climb a tree,
Wherever you go, it's always free,
In big, open spaces, I like to play football,
Muddy or grassy, I don't mind at all,
It's fun making dens in the woods,
Have you tried it? Everyone should!
Animals are great to watch scuttling around,
In the sky and the sea, or even the ground,
In autumn, there's conkers, in winter, there's snow,
In spring, there are flowers, in summer, sun shows,
There are beautiful things here on our planet,
Let's care for the environment, go out and protect it!

Ezra Dew (7)
Clyst Heath Nursery & Community Primary School, Clyst Heath

Nature Keeps Us Alive

Ten trees, swaying back and forth,
Twenty turtles, each going 1mph,
Thirty frogs, jumping into their pond,
Forty foxes, hunting for food,
Fifty falcons, flying north,
Sixty spiders, weaving webs and catching flies,
Seventy snakes, slithering in the African grasses,
Eighty octopuses, struggling to untangle themselves,
Ninety newts, mating with each other,
And one hundred of us in our county, planting flowers and food,
All of this keeps us alive,
Animals, plants, and food,
Nature keeps us alive.

Tymon Nadolny (8)
Clyst Heath Nursery & Community Primary School, Clyst Heath

My Little Seedling

My little seedlings are so tall and brave,
Making their way through these chilly months,
And into the early spring sun,
All apart from one.

My little seedling, why are you not growing?
There are no signs of your dainty leaves showing,
I have watered you, cared for you, and sung to you every night,
My little seedling, the sun shines bright.

Finally, as summer rolls in,
My little seedling,
You begin
To show.

Save wildlife,
We need to protect it,
And help it grow!

Gabriella Reece (10)
Clyst Heath Nursery & Community Primary School, Clyst Heath

Nature Bird

N ever give up,
A nd try to achieve your goals,
T ry to start simple and get harder,
U nderstand it takes time,
R each your goals,
E lephants are speechless,

A lligators are singers,
N ever feed alligators,
D eer are very cute,

B ats sleep through the day,
I ce is cold,
R obins have a red chest,
D olphins live in the water,
S heep live on a farm.

Amie Davey (8)
Clyst Heath Nursery & Community Primary School, Clyst Heath

Environment

- **E** xtinct animals are so pretty,
- **N** ature sometimes grows in the city,
- **V** ery large plants grow like weeds,
- **I** nsist to do a good deed,
- **R** ainforests are so big,
- **O** ver hills, live earwigs,
- **N** ectar helps the bees,
- **M** any sick fish come from the seas,
- **E** ating animals isn't nice,
- **N** ext time, eat rice,
- **T** ell everyone about the animals in danger.

Phoebe Rutter (8)
Clyst Heath Nursery & Community Primary School, Clyst Heath

Nature

Nature is all around us,
Every year, plants grow in the wilderness,
It is important to the world,
Not only because it is beautiful in spring,
But also because it is a home,
Or a habitat for the world's greatest creatures,
A lot of animals lose their homes,
Due to pollution, or trees being cut down,
More animals every year become endangered,
Due to the loss of their homes,
Please, heal the Earth.

Alice Kachali (9)
Clyst Heath Nursery & Community Primary School, Clyst Heath

Our Planet

O ur sun is a massive star,
U se sustainable products,
R ecycle correctly and please don't litter,

P ollution is bad for our environment,
L et's work together,
A team will help us get this job done,
N ature is amazing so try to connect with it,
E arth is important, so please keep it clean,
T rees keep us alive.

Taylor Scholfield (9)
Clyst Heath Nursery & Community Primary School, Clyst Heath

How To Save The World

Don't throw litter on the ground,
It could be eaten or found,
Ride your bike, don't drive your car,
Use a train if you need to go far,
Pick up your dog's doo-doo,
That's not nice for someone's shoe,
Don't climb trees or pick wild flowers,
Do whatever is in your powers,
Use a bag for life at Tesco,
We can do it everyone, let's go!

Poppy Morgan (7)
Clyst Heath Nursery & Community Primary School, Clyst Heath

Adder

A nimal prey, hide away, as I'm camouflaged so you don't see me pounce,
D emon eyes as I see something, as dangerous as a sharp blade,
D anger's ahead, it's unsafe to cross, as you'll see a flash of a shadow,
E nemies ahead, it's deadly, escape or die,
R ed eyes as light as a bright, dazzling light, lighting up the night sky.

Rory Hart (8)
Clyst Heath Nursery & Community Primary School, Clyst Heath

Oak Tree

O ld owls live in me, they love to rest and nest in me,
A corns grow on my branches, lots fall down, what are the chances?
K ing of the forest, it's a wise old owl,

T all like a mansion,
R oots grow high as a skyscraper,
E xcellent oxygen for my human friends,
E arth's best acorn bringer.

Gabriella Booth (7)
Clyst Heath Nursery & Community Primary School, Clyst Heath

Nature

N ature is everywhere, plants, grass, trees,
A nimals can be in danger, always respect nature,
T all trees have emerald-green leaves,
U sually the best place with nature is woods and huge jungles,
R eddish tummies are robins' tummies,
E arth is a colourful colossal golf ball.

Sebastian Czapiewski (8)
Clyst Heath Nursery & Community Primary School, Clyst Heath

Our Planet

The world is important for our ecosystems,
Especially our animals,
The winter or summer,
Our animals are important to us,
They care about us,
We too care about them,
The climate change is hot or cold,
We choose to be cold or hot,
The most important things are animals.

Alex Weissabel (8)
Clyst Heath Nursery & Community Primary School, Clyst Heath

Wildlife

W ater, we must save,
I nside and out,
L etting nature grow,
D ealing with climate,
L oving our environment,
I nhale and exhale,
F eeding all our plants,
E nvironmentally fun, here we come!

Sophia Axon (10)
Clyst Heath Nursery & Community Primary School, Clyst Heath

Insects

Worms are very wiggly,
And snails are very slow.
Grasshoppers are very bouncy,
Ladybirds are very fluttery,
And ants are very stuttery.
Beetles are very iridescent,
And crickets are very noisy.
Finally, woodlouse are very teeny weeny.

Marley Gould (7)
Clyst Heath Nursery & Community Primary School, Clyst Heath

The Robin

Oh, robin, so dear,
When you are here,
Reminds me that my loved ones are near,
Your wings are like an invisible cuddle,
From a huddle of loved ones in Heaven,
Oh, robin, so dear,
The comfort you bring,
When you are near.

Olivia Holingworth (8)
Clyst Heath Nursery & Community Primary School, Clyst Heath

Recycling World

P lease put your rubbish in the bin,
L isten to me now,
A nd put your recycling in the right bin,
N ot the brown bin,
E ven not the black bin,
T o save our Planet Earth!

Ted Elmer (6)
Clyst Heath Nursery & Community Primary School, Clyst Heath

Unicorn Is My Friend

I have a unicorn named Rosie,
She is nice and cosy,
When we go to bed,
She tells me stories so I can lay my head,
She tells me stories about the trees,
And how they make her feel free.

Ellie Pallister (6)
Clyst Heath Nursery & Community Primary School, Clyst Heath

Help The Earth

I cycle every day to school and back,
So the world gets more green,
This helps the Earth and the environment,
The rain helps us drink,
Rainforests help us breathe.

Oliver Ernest (7)
Clyst Heath Nursery & Community Primary School, Clyst Heath

The World Is Amazing And Big

The world is incredible and big,
And safe and amazing,
The world is green and blue,
We are so lucky to have this world,
The world is beautiful and calm.

Francesca Balch (5)
Clyst Heath Nursery & Community Primary School, Clyst Heath

My Eco Acrostic Poem

E co is so important because it impacts our lives,
N o matter how you do it, make sure our planet thrives,
V olcanoes have helped to keep our planet nice and cool,
I f you can get an electric car, it saves us using fuel,
R ain and snow help to produce water for animals and flowers,
O nly put recyclable things in the recycle bins, to save the council hours,
N ever litter because it's surprising how far it can go,
M aking sea creatures never show,
E -waste that ends up in landfill contributes to climate change,
N ew clean energy is a much better source, so exchange,
T ime for this poem to come to an end, I hope you get the message I'm trying to send.

Ruby Jenkins (10)
Cwmaber Junior School, Abertridwr

Oppy, NASA

I'm the rover sent to Mars to try and find out why
It's a lifeless, dusty planet, red and lonely in the sky,
Some scientists say that Mars was once a planet just like Earth,
With hills and water, greenery, life, and death, and birth,
But something happened, long ago, to turn her into this,
A lonely, red, and dusty planet in this dark abyss,
I stand on Mars and stare at Earth, that lovely blue and green,
That home we share together, on her too hard we lean,
We take her energy and gas, and decimate the seas,
We don't throw rubbish in the bin, and cut down all her trees,
So as I stand, alone up here, one thing I want to say:
Dear humans, far away on Earth, protect her every day.

Corin Williams-Baker (11)
Cwmaber Junior School, Abertridwr

The Environment

T he environment is being polluted,
H elp recycle things like plastic bottles,
E veryday things you can do help, even by picking up litter,

E very day, try to help by doing something small,
N ature is changing because we are not looking after the planet,
V ery little can help,
I n the sea, there is plastic pollution,
R emember to recycle,
O r reuse,
N o littering,
M ake crafts using plastic bottles,
E xtinction of animals might happen because of climate change,
N obody can do it by themselves, we all need to take part,
T ry to recycle as many things as you can.

Megan Davies (8)
Cwmaber Junior School, Abertridwr

Save The Animals

Hello, I'm an otter,
I'm slowly getting hotter,
Climate change is affecting me,
Please, oh please, save me.

Hello, I'm an elephant,
Unfairness? This is relevant,
Some humans keep hurting me for my tusks,
I need them for fighting, save me.

Hello, I'm a rattlesnake,
Here's a decision I need you to make,
Humans keep killing me for my skin,
Please, will you help me?

Let's start to not harm creatures,
They're all so very beautiful,
And maybe, maybe one day,
The world will become even better.

Alexa Davies (11)
Cwmaber Junior School, Abertridwr

Reduce, Reuse, Recycle

If we didn't have this planet, we all wouldn't exist,
To keep this planet green, like it always has been,
All of us need to try harder,
To reduce, reuse, recycle,
We all need to act with haste,
To reduce our food waste,
All of us need to try harder,
To reduce, reuse, recycle,
A little thing we could do,
Is reuse a bottle or two,
All of us need to try harder,
To reduce, reuse, recycle,
Think of what you put in the rubbish bin,
Can it go in the recycling?
All of us need to try harder,
To reduce, reuse, recycle.

Gracie Davies (10)
Cwmaber Junior School, Abertridwr

The World Falling Apart

Help the world, it's falling apart,
The climate clock is running out,
How do we help? What should we do?
The next generation is in doom.

Pollution is rising high,
People are starting to die,
How can we survive this lifetime?
Now people can't breathe as much as before the climate freeze.

Animals are going extinct and endangered,
Deforestation is starting to get even more dangerous for animals,
Icebergs melting is making polar bears struggle for food,
These animals may be doomed.

Evie Williams (11)
Cwmaber Junior School, Abertridwr

A Wonderful World

This world is wonderful,
But soon there will be no animals
For anyone to see,
Like the mountain gorillas,
And the African forest elephants,
And also the Amur leopard,
We must look after this world,
Or these animals will be extinct,
Plastic is blocking up our rivers,
We must protect the rainforest,
And stop climate change,
For those who come after
Can only dream of the lovely things we have seen.

Lowri Harding (9)
Cwmaber Junior School, Abertridwr

Our Planet

O ur planet is slowly dying,
U sed rubbish in the sea,
R ainforests are being cut down,

P lease help, have some responsibility,
L itter less, recycle instead,
A nimals need help before they become extinct,
N ature needs to stay beautiful,
E veryone can help, reduce, reuse, recycle,
T ogether we can save the Earth.

Seren Humphreys (8)
Cwmaber Junior School, Abertridwr

Being Eco-Friendly

E arth is my home,
C aring for it is all of
O ur responsibility,
F orests need conserving,
R ivers need to stay clean,
I ce caps keep melting,
E ndangered animals need protecting,
N ature needs our help,
D on't forget to reduce, reuse, recycle,
L ove this planet,
Y ou know what you need to do!

Hyrum Perry (8)
Cwmaber Junior School, Abertridwr

The Rainforest

Pitter-patter, the drops of rain fall on the leaves,
The frogs jump over fallen trees,
The humans laugh after they bash through the trees,
Elephants huff and puff with the breeze,
They say, "When is someone going to stop these thieves
From cutting down our trees?"
Then a jaguar leaps off a stiff branch and says,
"I will help you get rid of these thieves!"

Gracie Gould (10)
Cwmaber Junior School, Abertridwr

Climate Change

Climate change is here,
Rivers are overflowing,
Icebergs are melting,
Days are getting hotter,
What is going to happen to this world?
Why are people trashing it,
Instead of recycling,
Who is going to plant the trees?
Who is going to clean the seas?
Who is going to save the bees?
Make it us, please, please, please,
Make it us, let's save the world.

Freddie Evans (9)
Cwmaber Junior School, Abertridwr

The World Around Us

I barely see trees of green,
And red roses too,
But to make 2023 more eco,
I need a little help from you,

To make this year more eco
Is what I really want,
So let's clean up together,
From Rome to Vermont,

So, be sure to recycle plastic,
So the planet can be fantastic,
And also, never litter,
So Earth can be fitter.

Kian Hart (11)
Cwmaber Junior School, Abertridwr

Our Planet

O ur planet is dying,
U nless we act fast,
R ecycle as much as possible,

P rotect the environment,
L ook after our oceans,
A void air pollution,
N ature must be helped,
E xtinction must be stopped,
T ake a stand.

Evie Carben (7)
Cwmaber Junior School, Abertridwr

Big Green

Our world and animals are dying,
And going extinct,
Please stop getting rid of elephant tusks,
And getting rid of rhinos,
And stop pollution too,
It kills animals,
So stop polluting,
And stop getting rid of elephants and rhinos,
And animals.

Summer Smith Harris (8)
Cwmaber Junior School, Abertridwr

A River's Song

Inspired by The River's Story by Brian Patten

I remember when life was good,
I plunged out of my mountain origins,
Brushing reeds and pebbles,
Tiptoeing in trickles as rivulets joined me
On my downward journey, pulled by gravity,
Soon, I grew into a stream,
Battling mossy rocks, eroding channels,
A v-shaped scar on the landscape,
My youthful spirit erupts
As I become more fast-flowing,
My current flinging me up into the air
As I hurtled over the lips of rocks,
Sending spray up like thousands of tiny diamonds,
Into a curtain of dancing water,
Then my journey continued,
Calmer and quieter, I twisted and turned,
Having grown wider and deeper,
Ambling through lush fields,
From time to time, swelling and spilling my banks
With my wasted water.

I remember when life was good,
When kingfishers, like shimmering rainbows,
Dived head-first into my waters and
Armies of frogs serenaded me,
When water boatmen skated
Across my barely rippling surface,
It was a sweet time, a bygone time,
A time before mankind's oil crimes,
A time before factories,
Brick by gluttonous brick,
Pumped me full of poisons,
A time before foul plastics
Threatened my waters
And condemned my wildlife.

Children, come and find me, if you please,
For I am your inheritance,
Once, I danced to nature's tune,
But now mankind pulls the strings,
Come and help me, if you dare,
Reverse the legacy of humanity.

Libby Williams (8)
Garway Primary School, Garway

A River's Song

Inspired by The River's Story by Brian Patten

I remember when life was good,
Oozing through the sponge-like mossy bed,
As I brushed the hands of rocks,
Tenderly eroding them, bit by bit,
Rivulets joined me,
As I carved my way through the wild marshland,
Throwing myself into fast-flowing rapids,
Carefree, I blasted over the lips of rocks,
Blanketing everything in my path
With a wild, flying curtain of foam.

I remember when life was good,
Meandering through meadows, deep and wide,
From time to time, bursting out of my banks,
On calm days, otters lounged on my still waters,
Doggy-paddling downstream, as swans
Covered me like blankets with their majestic
Silver necks stretched out for all to see,
Dragonflies were my ballerinas,
Swiftly flapping their filmy wings,

As their enchanting, blue-green bodies
Flickered iridescently.

It was a sweet time, a bygone time,
A time before nutrient pollution caused
My waters to fill with suffocating algae,
A time before factories pumped their
Thick sludge into my arteries,
Voracious humanity grew, while I shrank,
Pollution ran rampant and
I am carefree no longer,
Children, come and find me, if you dare,
For I am your legacy,
Who would believe that my crystal-clear waters
Would be reduced to a wasteland?
My journey is now perilous.

Sophie Nicholls (9)
Garway Primary School, Garway

A River's Song

Inspired by The River's Story by Brian Patten

I remember when life was good,
When I trickled down mountainsides,
Young and energetic,
Eagerly tumbling down waterfalls,
Sending froth flying,
Then I changed, grew wide and deep,
Leisurely, I meandered through lush fields of green,
Occasionally bursting my banks.

I remember when life was good,
When fluffy pine martens scampered
Along my riverbank,
Shrieking their cat-like calls,
When small, wet frogs
Slid swiftly across my water,
But, best of all,
When, in a kaleidoscope of colour,
Kingfishers dipped their wings
Gently in my skin.

It was a sweet time, a bygone time,
A time before humanity hurtled their litter at me,
A time before I was filled with bric-a-brac,
Before factories scavenged for more room,
Their greediness overflowing,
Which left me cowering in dark corners,
Time over time, cities grew,
Factories grew, pollution grew,
Now the only living thing around me
Is a single strand of grass.

Throughout my lifetime, I have sorrowfully flowed,
Children, this is what your kind has made me,
Now I'm in a watery grave, except no soul cares,
You've insulted me, betrayed me,
So, children, find me if you wish,
But I won't be what you think,
And you will be devastated.

Lena Sparey (8)
Garway Primary School, Garway

A River's Song
Inspired by The River's Story by Brian Patten

I remember when life was good,
When I toiled and twined
Down loggy mountain moorlands and through valleys,
I started as a trickle of water,
Eroding myself pathways to run down,
As I grew into a stream,
I carved v-shaped valleys,
Before the pull of gravity
Eventually slowed me down,
Wider and deeper, I snaked
My way through lush meadows and farmland,
Sometimes, on a whim, bursting my banks.

I remember when life was good,
When majestic swans floated downstream
Like graceful ballerinas,
And mud-brown otters, smooth as silk,
Glided beneath my waters like a shark,
Intent on catching their prey.

It was a sweet time, a bygone time,
A time before factories tortured my
Once crystal-clear waters,
Suddenly, I became cluttered by gathering waste,
They spewed their disgusting saliva
On my now filthy, brown waters,
Thick, black, choking sludge
Poured its way down to drains,
And found its unknown way to my once lovely waters,
How I miss all the wonderful, beautiful wildlife,
Children, come and find me, if you wish,
I am your inheritance,
Your ancestors have poisoned me with their greed,
It's your time to shine, your time to act,
There is no time to waste.

Florence Fullbrook (8)
Garway Primary School, Garway

A River's Song

Inspired by The River's Story by Brian Patten

I remember when life was good,
Peeping out from my mountain range,
Eating rivulets, growing bigger and stronger,
Giggling, tickling rocks and carving river banks,
King of the v-shaped valley,
Building up speed, I raced the wind,
Studied the trees as down, down, down I fell,
I hurtled, plunged, roared,
Tumbled down waterfalls, then
Back to a calm current, I changed,
I grew calm and tranquil,
Worming my way through the countryside,
Occasionally bursting my banks.

I remember when life was good,
When elusive kingfishers
Partied like disco lights overheard,
When armies of tadpoles
Cascaded from their spawn,
Scattering under my lily pads,
Like ice skaters, water boatmen

Pirouetted across my surface,
It was a sweet time, a bygone time,
A time before factories expanded,
Smothering the light that once shone upon me,
A time before pollution rampaged
Through me like a killer virus,
And dangerous chemicals bullied me into submission,
Like clogged arteries, my once crystal-clear water
Filled with sludge.

Children, come and find me, if you dare,
I am your inheritance.

Alfred Simpson (8)
Garway Primary School, Garway

A River's Song

Inspired by The River's Story by Brian Patten

I remember when life was good,
I peeped out of my deserted home,
Bubbling and trickling,
Tickling the soft moss,
Rivulets fed me and nourished me,
I grew bigger and stronger,
Eroding the landscape,
Reaching thrilling cliff edges,
Where my wild current flung me,
Frothing and foaming, into the air,
Then down, down, down, onto the rocks below,
Otters, brown and sleek,
Wriggled and waggled through my calm, clean water,
Blue and orange kingfishers
Elegantly fluttered over my surface,
Stalking their prey,
Long-legged water boatmen
Paddled daintily across my skin,
It was a sweet time, a bygone time,

A time before humans tortured me,
Destroying my peaceful way of life,
A time before factories vomited
Their thick, oily sludge into me,
Like heartless monsters,
They choked me with horrible plastic.

Children, come and find me,
I am your legacy, a brown trickle of sludge,
I, who was a miracle of nature,
Have been turned into this!
Is this what you want to see?
Do you dare to help?
Do you dare abandon me?

Albert Simpson (8)
Garway Primary School, Garway

A River's Song

Inspired by The River's Story by Brian Patten

I remember when life was good,
When I flowed free,
Down the rocky mountainside,
Chiselling v-shaped channels,
Excitement filled me as my youthful spirit
Plunged head-first
Over the top of the rocky cliffs,
Thundering endlessly,
Then my nature changed,
As I stretched across flat grasslands,
Slowly weaving and wandering,
Wandering and weaving.

I remember when life was good,
When otters dived into me,
Their webbed feet like flippers,
Their elongated bodies,
When swans gracefully drifted downstream,
Their soft elegant wings tucked away,
It was a sweet time, a bygone time,
A time before factories exhaled their smoke,

Now, I choke on waste and junk,
Sludge and oil pour into my once-clear waters,
And poisons rob me of my oxygen.

Children, come to me, if you dare,
I am your inheritance,
I, who have flowed through history,
Free, fresh, pure, full of life,
Have been reduced to a rotting, toxic relic,
Will you help me become who I once was
Or will you let me perish?

Cordelia Siriwardena (8)
Garway Primary School, Garway

A River's Song

Inspired by The River's Story by Brian Patten

I remember when life was good,
Peeping out of my mountainous source,
Cheerfully flowing through biome after biome,
I toppled over moss-covered rocks,
Eroded the land into v-shaped channels,
Racing downward at the speed of light,
Juggling rocks as I went,
I curved and bent my way
Through forests, then meadows.

I remember when life was sweet,
When otters elegantly weaved
Through my crystal-clear waters,
And dragonflies levitated above my surface,
A flashing, fluttering of blue-green,
It was a sweet time, a bygone time,
A time before spluttering factories,
Brick by greedy brick,
Filled the air with their fumes,
A time before plastic and waste
Strangled and choked me.

Children, come and find me, if you dare,
I have journeyed for generations, yet
You have compromised me with your waste,
You have choked me, clogged me,
Turned me into an open sewer,
Destroyed my wondrous landscape,
Is this to be my demise?

Charlie Myhil (8)
Garway Primary School, Garway

Underwater Turtles

U nited Kingdom has quite a lot of turtles,
N ever kill turtles,
D on't sit on their shells,
E legantly moves,
R epresenting how important they are,
W ater has one billion bits of plastic,
A nd sometimes they're in danger,
T urtles have wonderful patterns,
E ven though turtles are small, try to avoid them,
R emember the turtles who have died,

T ry to remember their patterns,
U nderwater sea creatures, oh I love them,
R emember their marvellous patterns,
T ry to respect them,
L ies down in the littered ocean,
E nter the Big Green Poetry Machine.

Isla Woodhouse (7)
Garway Primary School, Garway

The Great Oak Tree

On an oak tree, there are beautiful leaves gleaming,
An oak tree is straight, long, tall and brown,
Remember the part of nature in the palm of the tree,
Two thousand loads of trunks are getting chopped off,
Represent the leaves that shine in the sun,
Enter the huge trees in the hills that are huge,
Enter the Big Green Poetry Machine,
Happy times may be in this tree,
Umbrellas on the tree, you always shimmer,
Miles of roots are under the ground,
On an oak tree, the wood is rough,
Roots are underground, very long,
Guide them through the sky like clouds,
Over the clouds, you may see them,
Yes, the mountains in the hills,
So long branches, so very long.

Teddy Fullbrook (6)
Garway Primary School, Garway

It Wasn't Always Like This

It wasn't always like this,
Before the humans came,
The trees and forests used to thrive,
And now beastly bulldozers devour forests with pleasure,
And plague my skies with fires.

It wasn't always like this,
Before the humans came,
The panda bear used to feast like a king,
On great bamboo trees,
But now they only have mere tree stumps.

It wasn't always like this,
Before the humans came,
The rhino used to rejoice like he had everything,
But now their lives are taken,
For the pleasure of an ivory necklace.

It wasn't always like this,
I'm only asking,
Why?

Annabel Atkinson (9)
Garway Primary School, Garway

Sloths Are Very Slow

S o slow, so very slow,
L oads of sleep,
O h, they hang off trees,
T hey sleep all day,
H orses are way faster,
S ome other animals are slow,

A sloth is very hungry,
R emember they're fluffy,
E very tree helps the sloths,

V ery, very hungry,
E very sloth is important,
R emember, they are very slow,
Y our rabbit is fluffy like a sloth,

S o do you know about sloths?
L oads of fluff,
O h, do you know about sloths?
W ow, sloths are amazing!

Louis Moulton (7)
Garway Primary School, Garway

The Poor Polar Bear

There was once a small polar bear,
He loved the Earth,
He really did care.

But slowly, his home was drifting away,
Because of the weather,
And the climate these days.

Until he became on his own,
Trapped on a small block of ice,
Far from his home.

He looked up to see lots of smoke,
All over the sky,
Because of blokes.

He was only a cub, only small,
Away from his mum,
No one to call.

We really need to look after this place,
Save it,
We're wiping out an animal race,

Let's look after our place,
Our planet.

Aden Evans (10)
Garway Primary School, Garway

The Jungle

Tall trees tower above dense shrubs,
Monkeys swing and joy it brings,
Snakes slither in their own sly way,
The rhythmic humming of the undergrowth
Resounds through the trees,
Then the river spoke,
"Toxic waste pulses through me,
I am plagued by plastic."
The trees murmur,
"Soulless metal monsters
Devour tree after tree,
Day after day."
Then, the oldest creature in the forest,
The giant tortoise, spoke,
"You know, it wasn't always like this,
There was a time when the trees
Were laden with delicious fruits."

Reuben Hill (9)
Garway Primary School, Garway

Nature Lover

N ever be unkind to the environment, love it,
A nd nature is in danger, they're dying, save them,
T ry and not hurt them, love them, keep them alive,
U nder danger, animals are in, give nature a chance,
R educe plastic to make sure they can breathe, it's lovely,
E scape animals from danger, nature is beautiful,

L ove it, some of the animals are extinct,
O ver in the Arctic, the ice is melting,
V ery many animals are dying,
E arth is important to us, look after it,
R esponsible for it.

Thea Probert (6)
Garway Primary School, Garway

Earth's Sad Soul

I see Earth's ice caps melting,
It fills me with despair,
There seems no way of halting
The rising waters everywhere.

The smell on Earth is awful,
Pollution has caused the stench,
You would think it would be unlawful,
Corporate profits are the wrench.

From my position, up in space,
I see what's going on,
Flooding, fires, heatwaves, storms,
Where has the old Earth gone?

People really should take care
Of all they have,
They're like locusts, taking what they want,
I hope they don't come to me.

Samuel Gwenter (9)
Garway Primary School, Garway

Flames Are Fought

F ire is spreading,
L ife is dying,
A ll because of global warming,
M ostly because of greenhouse gases,
E verything is burning,
S top the gases,

A fter the blaze,
R escue arrives,
E verything is smouldering,

F irefighters are heroes,
O ught to have a rest,
U nder the pressure of helping the world,
G reatness is awarded,
H atred is fought,
T hanks to all the heroes who fight the crisis.

Aiden Read (11)
Garway Primary School, Garway

My Adventure As A Polar Bear

Once upon a time,
Me and my siblings had fun,
Catching fish and swimming in the sapphire-blue sea,
But now it's only me.
My old glistening white fur is tangly,
Now I lie curled up in a ball,
While dirty brown water floods my iceberg,
Like a desperate fish, gasping for air.
It is very sad to see.
Sometimes, I wake up
To hear the icebergs calling for me,
Cubs yap as they drift out into the murky waters,
Souls of mums walk by,
Like soundless sighs.
Why are humans doing this?

Olive Johnson (9)
Garway Primary School, Garway

Do You Want A Planet?

Do you want a planet,
Where summers catch fire,
Winters cause deaths?
People say act in five years, they are liars,
But we need to act now and go on a quest.

Do you want a planet,
Where pollution kills fish?
Do you want the air to smell bad?
They say don't worry, but that's tash tish.
If the Stone Age was back, I would be glad!

So do you want a planet?
Let's all act together,
Everyone, act now,
Then the world will be better,
With one big, POW!

Mabel Jones (9)
Garway Primary School, Garway

Foxy Loxy

Foxy Loxy was howling in the moonlight,
Foxy was in the water,
The fox was in his bed,
Fox, you are a miracle,
Everyone was in their beds,
"Let's play," said Foxy Loxy,
Only Foxy Loxy was awake,
Foxy was in the woods,
Everyone went looking for him at night,
Everyone was happy when he returned,
"Look at how dark it is."
"Very dark," said Foxy Loxy,
"Very lovely, you are,"
Said Foxy,
Everyone was happy.

Ottilie Learmond (7)
Garway Primary School, Garway

The Ocean

Once, I was beautiful,
Once, I was flourishing with wildlife, like a cornucopia of fish,
Once, all animals lived in harmony,
Now I'm filled with despair, my fish are dying,
Once...
Now...
My water is dead,
I am drowning,
People dump their waste into my once-clean waters,
Plastic clogs up my estuaries, building an unnatural dam,
Killing my fish,
I am desolate,
I have dried up,
I am weeping,
I am drowning,
Why?

Malakai Longden Berg (9)
Garway Primary School, Garway

Save Our Trees And Flowers

E veryone, please don't cut
N ature and flowers, please save them,
V ines and trees, please don't pick,
I n the tree, might live something,
R ight around the tree,
O n the branches,
N uts aren't to pick, they're for squirrels,
M ighty and fierce, don't kill them,
E ven animals might climb and hide,
N ature is where they live,
T rees are to live not die.

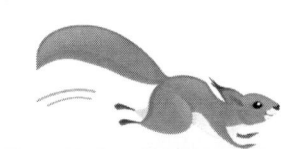

Ludo Probert (6)
Garway Primary School, Garway

Earth's Problems

My name is Earth,
I live in space,
It's a lovely place,
But they forget what I am worth,
Lots of people live on me,
They cut down trees,
And poison bees,
Even put plastic in the sea.

It makes me feel sad,
It makes me feel bad.

Icebergs are crumbling,
Penguins are stumbling,
Lions steal livestock
Because farmers steal land,
Which limits their habitat,
They need a hand,
I need help!

Samuel Rusling (9)
Garway Primary School, Garway

Nature

N ature is going extinct and we don't want that to happen because I love nature and other people do too,
A ll nature and animals need to be saved,
T ime is going fast and that means people are killing them fast,
U nder the sea, animals are getting killed,
R ound the world, in Africa, animals are getting killed,
E very single day, animals are getting killed and I don't like that, it makes me really sad.

Nicole Evans (6)
Garway Primary School, Garway

Pollution

I make up most of the world,
You swim in me,
You need me to survive,
Another form of me is ice,
You drink me,
I am the colour of the sky,
Fish live in me,
I am sometimes safe and sometimes dangerous,
I am being polluted,
My population is dying,
People use me as a rubbish bin,
I am rising and taking over the world,
I create cyclones and tropical storms,
What am I?

Answer: Water.

William Franklin (10)
Garway Primary School, Garway

Pollution In The Ocean

Sitting there, all by myself,
I think about the ocean,
Her lapping waves against the shores,
She's full of pollution.

Plastic bottles, pans and bags,
Clog up her merry waves,
Help her quickly! Help her now!
Before it's the end of her long, lonely days.

I feel the water on my feet,
But I hear an unpleasant sound,
I think it must be the ocean crying,
For she is very close to dying.

Ebenie Barreau (11)
Garway Primary School, Garway

The New Ocean

Long ago, my waves were dear,
Animals lived without any fear,
Turtles could swim without getting tangled in nets,
Fish would eat without ingesting plastic pellets.

I feel like a bin,
Full of rubbish and grime,
Pollution from oil spills and junk,
Make me feel ill all of the time.

I wish I felt better,
Like the good old days,
When fish could swim freely,
Through my clear, tall waves.

Ronnie Monaghan-Teale (9)
Garway Primary School, Garway

Trees

S ave our trees,
A n endangered tree,
V ery endangered trees on our planet,
E arth needs trees,

O ur trees need saving,
U nknown trees always falling,
R ainforests in trouble,

T ropical rainforests in trouble,
R ainforests are in danger,
E xtinct trees,
E xtinct leaves,
S ave our trees.

Libby Quan (7)
Garway Primary School, Garway

Earth

Earth is beautiful,
But it's falling,
Climate change and pollution
May take it down,
So what can we do to stop this mess?
Just let me explain,
The more we recycle,
The better it can be,
Pick up the plastics,
To help nature be
Safe and sound,
Let near-extinct animals
Have their dream,
So, let's save our planet,
Let nature live on.

Jack Monaghan-Teale (11)
Garway Primary School, Garway

Farming

The farmers are polluting the rivers, oceans, and green spaces,
Sloths are endangered, so are elephants and rhinos,
Valuable rainforest is getting chopped down to create farms,
The sun is burning onto our fruit and veg because of the gases we are churning out,
Crops are being lost to flooding,
And people are dying from starvation,
People are throwing rubbish around.

Rachel Pugh (9)
Garway Primary School, Garway

Wildlife

W hy do people litter? It makes me so sad,
I f you litter, I will be bitter,
L ots of animals are getting hurt,
D anger to animals' families and homes,
L ittering is super bad, help so I won't be sad,
I f you hurt animals, my heart will break,
F oxes can be saved,
E lephants do not like to be hurt.

Greta Hoare-Shields (7)
Garway Primary School, Garway

Penguin

There was once a baby penguin,
He loved his snowy land,
But, one day,
Something strange happened,
He went to go on an adventure
To see this strange world,
But, suddenly, the ice broke,
He was stuck, stranded,
He never wanted it to be this way,
But it is...
If climate change wasn't a thing,
He wouldn't be there.

Henry Morgan (10)
Garway Primary School, Garway

Wildlife Is Special

W ildlife shouldn't be harmed,
I f you don't act now, animals will die,
L iving creatures should be protected,
D on't hurt animals,
L iving creatures are special,
I am sad that animals are getting hurt,
F urry animals are getting killed for their fur,
E arth is a green planet.

Reuben Littler (7)
Garway Primary School, Garway

Pollution

The water flows with chemicals,
Oxygen submerged with plastic particles,
Dreams of rainforests standing
To protect the Earth from passing.

Climate change is warming,
Surely this is a warning,
Darkness is overwhelming,
Soon the Earth will fade,
The life before, drifting away,
As pollution surrounds the bay.

Harriet Plant (10)
Garway Primary School, Garway

The War Against Plastic

We dump and dump
Rubbish out to sea,
We kill and kill
Fish out at sea,
We lie and lie
About the rubbish
We pump out to sea.

Whales dying,
Numbers declining,
Ice caps melting,
Water overflowing,
Pollution increasing,
Government collapsing,
Under pressure
From this matter.

Daniel Caleb Evans (11)
Garway Primary School, Garway

Endangered Animals

We need to look after our wildlife,
Lots of sea and land animals are extinct,
And more are nearly extinct,
So be more helpful,
And save our animals,
The Arctic is getting warmer,
And animals are dying quickly,
So please help the poor helpless animals
To be strong and powerful,
So please help.

Thomas Hughes (10)
Garway Primary School, Garway

Giraffe

G iant giraffes have pretty leopard-print patterns,
I mpossible to reach their heads,
R each really high,
A nd don't chop down trees,
F unny when they eat the leaves greedily,
F unny necks,
E very day, they eat leaves and stuff them in their mouths.

Rosie Christopher (6)
Garway Primary School, Garway

Pollution

P oles are melting,
O cean levels are rising,
L ife is dying,
L ife is struggling,
U gly fumes in our air,
T oxic gases spill out over us,
I cebergs melting in the sea,
O ur home is disappearing,
N ow we need help.

Edward Morris (10)
Garway Primary School, Garway

Plants, Water, Animals

Plants blowing
Through the fields,
New ones growing,
The environment,
The power it yields.

Water swaying,
Flowing through,
Listen to what the birds are saying,
They're calling you.

Help your planet survive,
Be that one kind-hearted life.

Angelo-Valentino Cable (11)
Garway Primary School, Garway

A Burning Nightmare

All around me is a blazing fire,
The hot ash chokes the angry sky,
It's hard to breathe,
I call amongst the jungle of flames,
But no one replies...
My paws are wrinkled and burnt,
My fur is gone, only patches remain,
Will I ever escape this nightmare?

Molly Siriwardena (11)
Garway Primary School, Garway

Environment

Environment,
Oceans are being filled with plastic,
The action will be drastic,
Around the rubbish, fish are swarming,
All the ice caps are warming.

Deforestation,
It's a situation,
Water levels are rising,
To all, this is not surprising!

Layla Carter (11)
Garway Primary School, Garway

Oceans

O ceans are being hurt by plastic,
C oral reefs are being destroyed,
E very sea animal is dying,
A nd there is almost
N othing left,
S ave the ocean.

James Peacock (11)
Garway Primary School, Garway

Panda

P owerful and fierce,
A black and white teddy bear,
N ibbles on bamboo,
D ens in hollowed-out logs,
A beautiful animal going extinct because of our pollution.

Jacob Pugh (11)
Garway Primary School, Garway

Earth Wants To Be The Best

I am strong, I am big,
A meteor would scream if he saw my digs,
The red planet would lose
Because I have the roots,
I have the guns,
But the more I use
The more I die!

Gene Farr (10)
Garway Primary School, Garway

Our Earth

P erfect and beautiful,
L et nature be free,
A wonderful sight,
N ever kill nature,
E nvironment is brilliant,
T rees need saving.

Jacks Sparey (7)
Garway Primary School, Garway

Sea Turtle

A kennings poem

Egg layer,
Elegant swimmer,
Gorgeous creature,
Bags polluting,
Sadly dying,
Bag choker,
Sand nest,
Beautiful outlines,
Lovely species.

Kayleigh Cobourn (10)
Garway Primary School, Garway

The Horse

H ow do you gallop?
O n the green grass,
R un like the wind,
S potty and white,
E verywhere the horse goes.

Nerys Gwenter (6)
Garway Primary School, Garway

Save Turtles

A kennings poem

Elegant swimmers,
Wondrous creatures,
Sadly dying,
Beach lover,
Jellyfish eater,
Plastic eater.

Poppy Brown (9)
Garway Primary School, Garway

Recycling

R educe and make it smaller.
E nergy can be saved by recycling.
C arbon output must be reduced.
Y ou save our world by recycling.
C ycling to places instead of using a car is better for the environment.
L ook after your planet by recycling and reducing.
I am responsible for my own recycling.
N ever too old to change bad habits, so start recycling now.
G o do all these things to help our environment.

Vesper (8)
Haughton St Giles CE Primary Academy, Haughton

Crises

Should I starve or have something to eat?
Should I freeze or turn on the heat?

Should I sit in the dark or turn on the light?
Should I sleep or worry at night?

Should I complain or better contain?
I don't know what to do, do you feel it too?

The rising costs have made us suffer,
I can't believe it, but hope it won't get tougher.

We are all in this together,
So let's take care of each other.

Take care of your friends and neighbours,
Help out and do some favours.

Offer a shoulder or maybe some food,
God knows, supporting them will lift their mood.

Remember, this time will come to pass,
But the love your share and spread will last.

Abdullah Saud Mannan (10)
Holy Trinity CE Junior School, Wallington

Recycle

If you make potato mash,
Don't throw it in the trash,
Look around for glass,
It would make a good mast,
If your clothes get small,
Reduce, reuse, recycle,
Leave it at your neighbour's door,
The amount of rubbish we produce,
It's time we start to reduce,
Our oceans are flooded with plastic,
Even whales don't think its fantastic,
Reduce, reuse, recycle,
Before you put the printer on,
Think of the tree that has just gone,
If your sofa gets too old,
With lots of little holes,
Reduce, reuse, recycle,
The recycling centre is the place,
So at home, you can have more space,
Reduce, reuse, recycle.

Maximilian Zatik (10)
Holy Trinity CE Junior School, Wallington

Plastic Is Bad

Time goes past,
There at last,
A little girl holding a thick,
Non-reusable,
Plastic water bottle
Skipped along the filthy road
Lined with cardboard and caps,
Paper and maps,
Plastic and broken glass.
She was on her way to her friend's house,
Skipping as she passed.
Finally, she arrived,
Buzzing and alive,
Her friend looked at her, horrified
At the sight of a bottle
With the lid on tight.
"Plastic," she said,
Shaking her head,
And snatched it from her hands.
"Use reusable,
The options are choosable,

Come on, be wise,
And then you'll realise,
Reusable is the best."

Daisy Davies (10)
Holy Trinity CE Junior School, Wallington

Don't You Care?

Imagine,
Sabretooth tigers on the grass floor,
Eating food and going *roar!*
What a shame they are extinct,
Come, sit down, and have a think,
Let's talk about other things,
How about rubbish inside the bin?
Come on, plastic takes ages to fade,
Soon a whole world of plastic will stay,
Even though we had a long warning,
That didn't stop us from creating global warming!
And the energy prices are soaring,
Now, one last thing about chopping trees,
There are no more homes for bumblebees,
Whoever made this sheet, I'll talk to them later,
Since this whole sheet is made of paper!

Finley Styles (10)
Holy Trinity CE Junior School, Wallington

The Bear's Last Stand

The sun is blaring,
My heart is tearing,
As the sun heats up,
My home melts in the day,
As the ice caps lay,
I think I can say,
They'll be gone in May.

I've not eaten for weeks,
Don't know where I can sleep,
I'm feeling quite weak,
Nowhere to seek.

I fear the end,
Something no one can mend,
It's here,
The death of a predator you'll fear,
Death is here, here, here,
Now I fear,
My death is here.

Sam Hunter-Brook (9)
Holy Trinity CE Junior School, Wallington

Save Our Lovely Planet

It's important to look after our planet,
It's the only one we've got,
We must protect our planet,
It doesn't take a lot.

Turn off your light,
Don't get a fright,
Switch off your devices
To help end this crisis.

Don't waste water,
Only use what you need,
With any left over,
Plant a seed.

Walk to school,
Or ride your bike,
Leave the car at home,
And go on a hike.

Animals are suffering,
And crying out for help,

Their habitats around them
Are beginning to melt.

Jack Walton (10)
Holy Trinity CE Junior School, Wallington

Mother Nature

Back in the day,
When nobody cared,
Everybody littered,
Mother Nature was scared.

Now, thanks to scientists,
And people who were brave,
There's more sustainable living,
Mother Nature can be saved.

And, although it's not as bad as before,
You still see a lot of plastic,
So pick it up wherever you can,
A world without litter? Fantastic!

So, in the future,
Avoid pollution,
And, together,
We'll find a solution!

Robyn Lang (10)
Holy Trinity CE Junior School, Wallington

Dreams

Ever since I was little, this has been my dream,
I will always wake up to the sunshine on my face,
Saying my greetings to the Earth where I rest,
Trash everywhere on the ground, nowhere near the bins,
Trees on the floor, animals being extinct,
I wanted to stop this once and for all,
Before more trees fall, before all trees fall,
I need you to help me to stop this catastrophe,
Please, oh please, stop this catastrophe.

Betina Khoobyar (10)
Holy Trinity CE Junior School, Wallington

The Bad Tiger In The Forest

In the forest, where all the animals play and rest,
There was a tiger who thought he was the best,
He was a liar, but nobody cared,
Because his stripes looked cool like fire.
And one day, he destroyed a tree,
And hit a bee,
And he knew that, one day,
He would have to pay,
So, three months later,
He had to change his behaviour,
So he planted some trees,
And he saved the bees.

Sydney-Rose Still-Hibbert (10)
Holy Trinity CE Junior School, Wallington

Save Earth

There is a bin over there,
It's just not fair,
People can't put things in the bin
And it's creating a din,
There's arguments and fights,
And it's just not right,
So I will help save the Earth,
Before there are no more births,
Even you should help save Earth because that is good,
Being good is how you should,
Save Earth and don't litter!

Jasmine D'Souza (9)
Holy Trinity CE Junior School, Wallington

Climate Can Change

You know you wanna stop climate change,
But people can't decide,
People want the Earth to be clean,
Although, some people disagree,
When you look at the beautiful streams,
And want the Earth to be beautiful like your dreams,
Don't litter,
You'll just be bitter,
You'll love a good ride,
But you can't leave Earth aside.

Abrar Gamaleldin (10)
Holy Trinity CE Junior School, Wallington

The Red In Flanders Fields

In Flanders Fields, the poppies grow,
Rocking in the wind, to and fro,
The wonderful dead
Rest respected in their beds,
If only I could see you again,
I'd give you my heart for one hug, my friend,
In Flanders Fields, you lie in peace,
In your heart, RIP,
In Flanders Fields, poppies grow,
Stone crosses lined in a row.

Ethan Vass (9)
Holy Trinity CE Junior School, Wallington

Look And Think

Look at the cars and pollution,
How do we find a solution?
The world is dying,
Our trees are crying,
And can start now,
Just turning the power
Off for one short hour
Can start,
The animal numbers begin to heal
When we eat less meaty meals,
Just stop and look,
Read this book
To learn how to save the world.

Felix White (10)
Holy Trinity CE Junior School, Wallington

Animals

Animals, animals, how do they feel?
Put yourself in their shoes,
And then you'll see!

Animals, animals, are they nice?
Indeed they can be,
But have a bit of spice!

- **A** rmadillo,
- **N** arwhal,
- **I** guana,
- **M** agpie,
- **A** lbatross,
- **L** ion,
- **S** nake.

Ava Brook (10)
Holy Trinity CE Junior School, Wallington

The Creatures Of The Rainforest

Through the trees,
In the breeze,
Lay a sleeping tiger,
Who thought he was better than the rest,
Even though he wasn't the best,
The truth is, he was a bit of a pest,
He knew, one day,
He would have to pay
For the time he cut down one of the trees in the bay,
But nobody cared, nobody would say!

Lillian Katat Cheetham (9)
Holy Trinity CE Junior School, Wallington

Nobody Should Litter

Why do they do it?
Why should they do it?
Littering is wrong, incorrect,
Nobody has the right to litter,
He does not do it,
She does not do it,
I do not do it,
So you should not do it,
But they still do it,
They still do it,
But, oh, why?
Please don't do it.

Beatrice Merivale (10)
Holy Trinity CE Junior School, Wallington

Nature

Oh, nature, without you, we'll be a failure,
Oh, nature, beautiful nature, our mother and nurturer,
Oh, nature, our beautiful nature, we thank you for your nurture,
We need your food to live,
You're too good to be true,
But we love you,
Oh, nature, we thank you for your nurture.

Mohamad Sidibe (10)
Holy Trinity CE Junior School, Wallington

Our Rainforest

Through the bushy trees,
Lies the rainforest,
Lies a fearless tiger
Coming to get his prey,
Then the spider creeps out
For his prey too,
But then, a sound,
It was a chainsaw,
And it was cutting down
One of the animal's homes.

Emily-Rose Tindle (9)
Holy Trinity CE Junior School, Wallington

Recycling

Reduce, reuse, and recycle,
These are words that we all know,
Glass, paper, plastic and tin,
Can be separated into your recycling bins,
We must start now,
We can't wait,
Quick, or it will be too late.

Nysa Ray (9)
Holy Trinity CE Junior School, Wallington

A Greenery Scene

One sun, always shining,
Never tired, not a single day off,
Many trees, their bodies always still,
Not daring to make a move,
Their leaves always in action,
Trying to dodge the hitting wind,
Flowers, making people's days,
Always attracting the bees,
But there's a problem, they slowly start fading away,
Slowly dying,
No one taking enough action,
Still doing their one job, giving us oxygen,
Keeping us alive, while dying,
I love nature,
Nature loves me,
If you love nature,
Nature will love you too.

Toochi Nwagbo (9)
Prince Edward Primary School, Sheffield

Nature Is My Mother

I stand by and watch her fall,
I'm desperate to do something, anything at all,
But what could a tree do?

Nature is my mother,
She cares for me,
I care for her.

But all I can do is watch, watch her scream,
And tackle the injustice of her world,
All alone.

She slowly loses her beauty,
As they inject her with poison,
It seeps through her skin, ripping it, damaging it,
But what could I do?

Nature is my mother,
Slowly losing everything she owns,
From her plants, to the trees, the trees to the animals, the animals to her family,
But I still stand.

She gives to the world,
But all she gets back
Is venom seeping through her skin.

With time, she grows weak and helpless,
This is when I've had enough,
I gather my friends, my family,
And we don't do any harm,
Instead, we protect her,
My Mother Nature.

The harm retreats,
Scrambling frantically,
Danger is gone.

I embrace her in an everlasting hug,
Mother is back!

A tree does many,
Many things for Mother,
Even by standing still,
They don't know,
But that's okay,
For my mother,

For my mother,
For my mother is nature,
And nature is my mother.

Esther Nwagbo (10)
Prince Edward Primary School, Sheffield

Nature's Wonders

Ponds are as blue as sapphires,
Ducks quack happily in the water,
Trees flowing,
Birds chirping,
The sun is red, red because it's a floating ruby in the sky,
Clouds are diamonds in the titanic blue sky,
Grass is emerald, emerald and pure,
Joyful people running all over the place,
Birds humming a tune all over again,
Fresh air is a dome of nature and happiness,
Graceful deer hop around with freedom,
A place where people don't pay fees,
A place where people can be happy and free.

Chimamanda Okoroafor (8)
Prince Edward Primary School, Sheffield

Turtles

Earth is my home,
We need to take care of our world,
I like to swim in the sea,
We need to recycle the plastic,
So I don't get sick.

I like swimming a lot,
I like it so much,
I never want to get out.

Help the world to save the animals,
Save the rainforest,
Save our oceans,
So turtles like me can swim!

Amen Messam (5)
Prince Edward Primary School, Sheffield

Nature

Nature is green,
Make it grow,
Make the world healthy,
If pollution keeps on going,
If people keep cutting down trees,
Then I won't be alive,
Do you know that trees use carbon dioxide
And bring out oxygen?
Let's make pollution extinct.

Praise Shodeinde (10)
Prince Edward Primary School, Sheffield

Let's Change The World

Let's change the world,
So it be told,
Stop throwing litter,
And don't act bitter,
Let's recycle our rubbish,
And take good care of our fish,
No dumping garbage in the sea,
And let's protect the buzzing bees,
Let's bike or purchase electric cars,
Let's give our environment a chance,
Please do not disturb nature,
Stop cutting down trees and let's start reusing paper,
Let's reuse our shopping bags,
Like Santa, who reuses his sacks!

Ruben Thurairatnam (8)
Rokeby School, Kingston Upon Thames

North Pole

I am a penguin,
I waddle and I walk on two feet,
I do not like people calling me meat.

I'm a whale,
And I do not get down and obey,
I swim free in the depths of Antarctica,
My blubber is warm like cool rubber.

I'm an Arctic wolf,
As some call me the lone wolf,
I am very wild,
Mostly self-styled,
Stop hunting me down for your town.

I'm a polar bear,
I am very aware,
What hunts me down,
I'm dying in age but I still have rage.

We are all animals,
We stand together from beak to fur,
And we all have the same dream.

Niamh Hirst (9)
Shocklach Oviatt CE Primary School, Malpas

Why?

Swimming in the sea,
Fish swim through me,
The coral is dead,
Sharks no longer live,
I swim through rubbish now,
Not clear blue ocean,
Dying of starvation,
Plastic is the reason,
Why are they doing this to us?

Proud and majestic,
I walk through my forest,
But I'm all alone,
Tiger blood splatters the trees,
Tiger bone wine in shop windows,
Oil palms planted where my cubs once walked,
Shot, made into skin rugs,
Greed is the reason,
Like the white rhinos,
Why are they doing this to us?

I stomp through the jungle,
Cattle now run where we used to swing,
Roads were built, our trees were destroyed,
No family or friends now swing with me,
No trees, no family, no home,
If nothing can be done,
You will see the last of us,
Why are you doing this to us?

Sophie Lloyd (11)
Shocklach Oviatt CE Primary School, Malpas

The Ocean

I see plastic everywhere I look,
It upsets me because,
One day, I could be in it,
The ocean used to be so calming,
But now it is just a pile of gunk,
We get caught in nets and we die,
Some of us never return,
One day, my brother went off,
Never to return,
I thought he could've got caught in a net,
I felt so down, I have no family,
I walk through the kelp,
I see a bright light,
It's my brother,
More and more of us are dying,
If you help, we will have more,
That's all I have to say.

Sophia Whittle-Jones (10)
Shocklach Oviatt CE Primary School, Malpas

Save The Planet

Soon, the trees will have no leaves,
And the animals will have fleas,
The birds won't fly in the sky,
You won't see them pass by,
The turtles won't swim in the sea,
Neither will you and me,
The ocean is a pile of junk,
The plastic has all sunk,
The world has started to yelp,
But yet, we have not given it help.

Eve Goggins (10)
Shocklach Oviatt CE Primary School, Malpas

Turtles

Swimming, swimming,
Bright blue seas are glimmering,
One by one, they're gone,
Paddling, paddling,
And through the bright blue sea,
The sad-looking fish begin to flee,
Bright green turtles swimming in the sea,
They won't be able to swim with you and me.

Annabel Burnett (10)
Shocklach Oviatt CE Primary School, Malpas

Polar Bears On Earth

Polar bears are dying,
Trying to survive in the wild,
The ice caps are melting,
Save the cubs from global warming,
Their food is dying,
Help them,
Or there will be no polar bears on Earth.

Eva Nicholas (9)
Shocklach Oviatt CE Primary School, Malpas

Panda

P lease save our pandas,
A nd we love pandas,
N o killing pandas,
D isappearing pandas is a no,
A nd save pandas.

Elliot Williams (8)
Shocklach Oviatt CE Primary School, Malpas

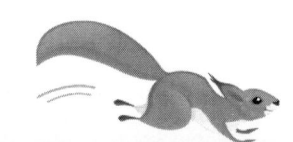

Polar Bear

P olar bears' lives have nearly ended,
O n the ice, it is hard for the polar bears to stand because it is cracking,
L onely polar bear lost its cubs,
A way their life goes,
R iding stuff and walking are much better,

B eing sad when they are gone,
E ncouraging people to stop driving,
A bit of rubbish could kill an animal,
R ipped plastic means an animal could eat it.

Amy Kingdon (8)
St Nicholas CE Primary School, Henstridge

Eco Poem

E nter a world of litter picking,
C leaning out the ocean,
O cean animals need space so they don't hit litter,

C aring for animals is important,
O ceans need cleaning,
U nder all of the rubbish on Earth,
N aughty people litter,
C aring for the world,
I n the eco council, we pick up litter to stop landfill,
L ittle bits of plastic can kill animals.

George Morgan (7)
St Nicholas CE Primary School, Henstridge

Eco Council

E nter a world of litter picking,
C are for the animals,
O ceans need clean space,

C are about others,
O ther people pick up other people's rubbish,
U se those litter pickers,
N ever leave litter around,
C an do is what we do,
I t is not good for the environment,
L itter is not good for the animals.

Maisie Bartlett (9)
St Nicholas CE Primary School, Henstridge

Rescue Animals

R escue animals,
E ncourage people to help animals,
S ave them,
C are for them,
U nder pressure and dying,
E verybody care for them,

A nimals in danger,
N eed to help them,
I love animals,
M eant to take care of them,
A nimals need help,
L ike to care for them.

Scarlett Ricketts (7)
St Nicholas CE Primary School, Henstridge

Sea Animals

S ea animals,
E veryone stop littering,
A n animal will be hurt by your litter,

A sea animal is endangered,
N ever litter,
I will watch you if you litter,
M e, I will never litter,
A n animal will be hurt if you litter, so please don't,
L ittering should stop,
S top littering!

Maddie Elliott (8)
St Nicholas CE Primary School, Henstridge

Squirrel

S quirrels, red, grey, and black,
Q uestions you may wonder,
U nderground is where they lie,
I see it now, a world of red and black,
R ed squirrels are dying,
R un, run! Far, far away,
E very red squirrel still joins their ancestors,
L ower and lower their numbers drop,
S o, save the squirrels!

Jake Stanley (9)
St Nicholas CE Primary School, Henstridge

Penguins

P enguins need help,
E nvironment work is happening,
N ature needs help,
G radually, the penguins will lose their numbers,
U nfortunately, the penguins will be extinct,
I ce is melting,
N ow, please help,
S ad the penguins will pass away.

Alfie Mckenna (8)
St Nicholas CE Primary School, Henstridge

The Earth

T he Earth is important,
H unters get food from the Earth,
E arth is where we live,

E arth is where animals and people
A re all around,
R emember the Earth,
T he Earth is sunny and windy,
H ungry people get food from the planet.

Scarlett Moore (8)
St Nicholas CE Primary School, Henstridge

Animals

A nimals are in danger,
N o littering, it will go in the sea,
I am making the animals better,
M ake the animals healthy,
A nimals like red pandas are in danger,
L et the animals know you,
S ave the seas and the animals for us to enjoy.

Summer Groves (7)
St Nicholas CE Primary School, Henstridge

Animals

A nimals are becoming extinct,
N ature is their home,
I f you drop rubbish, it is bad,
M ake something for them to live,
A nimals need help,
L itter is deadly for animals,
S ome squirrels are stealing from red squirrels.

Logan Sunley (8)
St Nicholas CE Primary School, Henstridge

Lovely Nature

N ature is really peaceful all around,
A nd all the grass swaying around,
T he trees are swaying all around,
U se the trees to get yummy apples,
R oots growing as tall as the trees,
E nough to be as tall as a giant.

James Sparshott (7)
St Nicholas CE Primary School, Henstridge

Forest

F orests have a lot of trees,
O n the trees, you can see green leaves,
R ocks could roll over to you,
E verywhere, there could be animals,
S ome people pick up animals in the forest,
T rees are all around you.

Kenny Smith (8)
St Nicholas CE Primary School, Henstridge

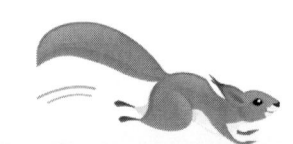

Animals

A nimals are in danger,
N eed to help them, we do,
I love penguins,
M y mum loves helping penguins,
A lot of animals need help,
L ike red pandas, red squirrels,
S mall animals also need help!

Esme Morris (8)
St Nicholas CE Primary School, Henstridge

Endangered Species

S pecies, our animals,
P recious animals should never die,
E veryone should look after species,
C an do is what we need to do,
I love species,
E ndangered, they are,
S oon, species will die.

Lucas Cole (7)
St Nicholas CE Primary School, Henstridge

Turtles

T aking plastic all out,
U p from the ocean's bottom,
R opes entangled,
T ry to clean the sea,
L ife could be better,
E nvironment,
S ea needs to stay clean for us all.

Freddie Windsor (7)
St Nicholas CE Primary School, Henstridge

Our Planet Needs Our Help

The planet is getting hotter,
And the sea is full of plastic,
We need to help the Earth,
And stop littering,
We should all help and stop polluting,
We need to recycle to help the environment,
Save our planet!

Ronny Whitney (8)
St Nicholas CE Primary School, Henstridge

Pandas

P lease help endangered animals,
A nimals must survive,
N ever not help them,
D angerous things will happen to them,
A nimals need our love,
S ave the pandas.

Iesha Peckover (7)
St Nicholas CE Primary School, Henstridge

Litter

P lease help,
L end us litter-pickers,
A nd the Earth is warming up,
S omeone help,
T ime is ticking,
I t's hurting the Earth,
C an you help?

Isaac George New (8)
St Nicholas CE Primary School, Henstridge

What Am I?

It has a pair of wings,
It has bright yellow and black stripes,
They are small creatures,
They can keep flowers alive,
And because of this, they are important.

Answer: A bee.

Mckenzie Murphy (8)
St Nicholas CE Primary School, Henstridge

Save The Trees

T rees are not supposed to be chopped down,
R educe the amount of paper waste,
E veryone loves trees,
E verybody gets oxygen from trees,
S ave the trees!

Toby Bowden (8)
St Nicholas CE Primary School, Henstridge

Nature

N ature,
A calm place to be,
T he trees wave at me,
U nstoppable animals are free to roam,
R eally cool animals,
E veryone save our world.

Grace Windsor (9)
St Nicholas CE Primary School, Henstridge

Litter

L ooking all around us,
I love to be everywhere,
T rash everywhere,
T ogether forever,
E nvironment,
R ubbish hurts us.

Samuel Hardie (8)
St Nicholas CE Primary School, Henstridge

School

The school is important and caring,
School is fun,
Being kind,
Also, we show perseverance,
Special at school,
What we do is look after our Earth.

Oliver Moult (7)
St Nicholas CE Primary School, Henstridge

Endangered Animals

Stop littering if you care about our Earth,
Red pandas and more animals are endangered,
You need to help me and my team,
Help and save the planet.

Alyssa Mortley (7)
St Nicholas CE Primary School, Henstridge

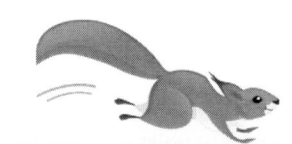

Wild Wind
A kennings poem

Blowing cobwebs,
A destroyer,
Paper stealer,
Rubbish taker,
Bin destroyer,
Blow blaster,
Balloon taker,
Fence breaker.

Archie Parsons (8)
St Nicholas CE Primary School, Henstridge

Cats

C ats run,
A nd never come,
T error comes to them, paws pricked,
S ites were full of rubbish, cats run.

Jimmy Hughes (7)
St Nicholas CE Primary School, Henstridge

What Am I?

I am everywhere,
I am nature,
Climate changes warms me,
I am mainly water.
What am I?

Answer: Earth.

E Hancock (8)
St Nicholas CE Primary School, Henstridge

Oh, Dear Rainforest

Oh, dear rainforest, I have something to say,
I was watching from my window,
And I wonder every day,

1000 more trees were cut down again,
When will it stop?
I really wonder when,

With colour, you are filled,
But cut down for a place to build,

You grow beautiful plants and flowers,
That get trampled on by buildings and towers,

For lots and lots of animals,
They can call you home,

A place they love and cherish,
A place they like to roam,

Sometimes, you're cut down to be made into paper,
Sometimes, you're destroyed by fumes and other vapours,

I know that you're the prime source for someone to deforest,
I'm really sorry, yes, I am,
Oh, dear rainforest.

Agnes Obi (10)
The Mount School, York

The Bumblebee

I fly high above the sky,
Yes, it's true, not a lie,

I leave a whispy trail behind,
I buzz around in my mind,

Hearing my wings as I fly,
Not caring or knowing why,

I do not bite but I sting,
Even though I never win,

Through the rain, I fly,
Even though I might die,

Through the thunder, through the rain,
People don't think I'm in pain,

Finally, a place to rest,
It's definitely the best.

Phoebe Murgatroyd (10)
The Mount School, York

Plastic

A kennings poem

No thank you, plastic,
Your change is so drastic,
You're a...
Turtle killer,
Fish murderer,
Countryside ruiner,
Street litterer,
Crop destructor,
Chicken choker,
Micro-plastic maker,
Person tripper,
Seal strangler,
Multi-use trasher,
Single-use encourager,
Recycling hater,
But, above all,
You're the end of the world.

Clementine Myatt (10)
The Mount School, York

The Amazon

The Amazon lies full of predators and prey,
You can seek the sound of wildlife all around,
The Amazon, it waits, filled with arguments and debates,
To protect its flowing waters and four humongous quarters,
It's ever so amazing, you could see a leopard dozing,
Now back to its insides, and everlasting pride,
For the animals that sleep, but I'm telling you, never dare to take a peep,
For venomous snakes and deep, deep lakes,
But research the kapok tree, it's the tree I'd like to see,
The showers and rainfalls glitter, and a teeny, tiny critter sits there, feeling important,
For this is the Amazon,
So protect its lands and wildlife bands,
And maybe, just maybe, you'll see a sloth in a tree above the cloudy cloth,
And there's so much more, I bet now you want to explore!

Imogen R (8)
Widmer End Pre School, Widmer End

Don't Make The Polar Bears Cry

Our ice caps are shrinking,
The ozone has a hole,
The forest fires are stinking,
It really hurts my soul,
We need to help our planet,
Here are some things we can do:
Don't leave the lights on,
Do your washing on cold,
Don't make the polar bears cry.

Morgan Birchall (11)
Woolston Brook School, Padgate

Planting Some More

Please don't cut down our trees,
It isn't very nice,
Our planet is on its knees,
So I'll give you some advice,
We need trees to breathe,
Let's plant more and more,
Machines need to leave,
Let's show them the door.

Riley Byrne (8)
Woolston Brook School, Padgate

The Polar Bear

Our polar bear is sad,
Because nobody helps her,
She is mad,
The ice caps are melting,
Help the polar bear,
Stop polluting her home!

Olivia Parkes (8)
Woolston Brook School, Padgate

YOUNG WRITERS INFORMATION

We hope you have enjoyed reading this book – and that you will continue to in the coming years.

If you're the parent or family member of an enthusiastic poet or story writer, do visit our website **www.youngwriters.co.uk/subscribe** and sign up to receive news, competitions, writing challenges and tips, activities and much, much more! There's lots to keep budding writers motivated!

If you would like to order further copies of this book, or any of our other titles, then please give us a call or order via your online account.

Young Writers
Remus House
Coltsfoot Drive
Peterborough
PE2 9BF
(01733) 890066
info@youngwriters.co.uk

Join in the conversation!
Tips, news, giveaways and much more!

YoungWritersUK   YoungWritersCW   youngwriterscw

Scan me to watch The Big Green video!